The toys we play with

This edition first published in 2006
by The Evans Publishing Group
2A Portman Mansions
Chiltern Street
London
W1U 6NR

British Library Cataloguing in Publication data.
A catalogue record for this book is available from the British Library.

Printed in Hong Kong by New Era Printing Company Ltd

ISBN 0 237 53130 5
13 digit ISBN (from January 2007) 978 0 237 53130 0

ACKNOWLEDGEMENTS:
Editorial: Louise John
Design: D.R.ink
Production: Jenny Mulvanny

PHOTOGRAPHS: Michael Stannard, except for the following:

Pages 8-9: baby with mobile (Early Learning Centre), early rattle (Private Collection/Bridgeman Art Library, London); page 13: Emprie State puzzle (Waddingtons); page 15: Javanese puppeteer (Robert Harding Picture Library); page 21: baseball and glove (The Image Bank); page 23: Victorian doll (The Bridgeman Art Library).

The authors and publishers would like to thank the following for their kind help with the objects photographed for this book: John Lewis department store, Early Learning Centre, The Entertainer, Beaties, The Kitestore, Boots, Gillian Richards Dolls Houses and SBS, Yate. Thanks to LEGO Dacta for permission to show LEGO® pieces and models on page 10.
Based on the original edition of The Toys We Play With published in 1997

A very special thank you to:
Lorna and the staff and children at the Brighton Street Nursery, Bristol, and specifically to our models there: Bláthain Callaghan (page 9), Flynn Conolly (page 7, middle) and Shakir Simpson (page 7, 8).
A big thank-you to Peter Bentley, Julia O'Neill and the pupils of Westbury-on Trym CE VC Primary School, and our models there: Sarah Hurt (page 24), Joshua Jefferies (pages 7, 19), Darren Joseph (pages 14, 19), Nishil Patel (pages 21, 24), Sofia Rahim (pages 10, 18, 19) and Ruth Wintle (pages 18, 21). Thanks also to Rosie Crews (cover and pages 14, 15).

Artworks and models:
Sue Woollant/Graham-Cameron Illustration Agency for border artworks on cover and inside, eye-opener logo and artworks on pages 8, 15 and 17; Mike Stannard for models on pages 11, 17 and 27; and Claudia Pagliarani for the artworks on pages 13 and the "make a glove puppet" models on page 14.

The toys we play with

Sally Hewitt and Jane Rowe

Evans

About this book

The LOOK AROUND YOU books have been put together in a way that makes them ideal for teachers and parents to share with young children. Take time over each question and project. Have fun learning about how all sorts of different homes, clothes, toys and everyday objects have been designed for a special purpose.

THE TOYS WE PLAY WITH deals with the kinds of ideas about design and technology that many children will be introduced to in their early years at school. The pictures and text will encourage children to explore design on the page, and all around them. This book will help them to understand some of the basic rules about why toys are made from specific materials and are a certain shape, and why they are suited to being played with in a particular way. It will also help them to develop their own design skills.

The 'eye opener' boxes reveal interesting and unusual facts, or lead children to examine one aspect of design. There are also activities that put theory into practice in an entertaining and informative way. Children learn most effectively by joining in, talking, asking questions and solving problems, so encourage them to talk about what they are doing and to find ways of solving the problems for themselves.

Try to make thinking about design and technology a part of everyday life. Just pick up any object around the house and talk about why it has been made that way, and how it could be improved. Design is not just a subject for adults. You can have a lot of fun with it at any age - and develop artistic flair and practical skills.

Contents

The toys we play with

There are lots of **different** sorts of **toys**.

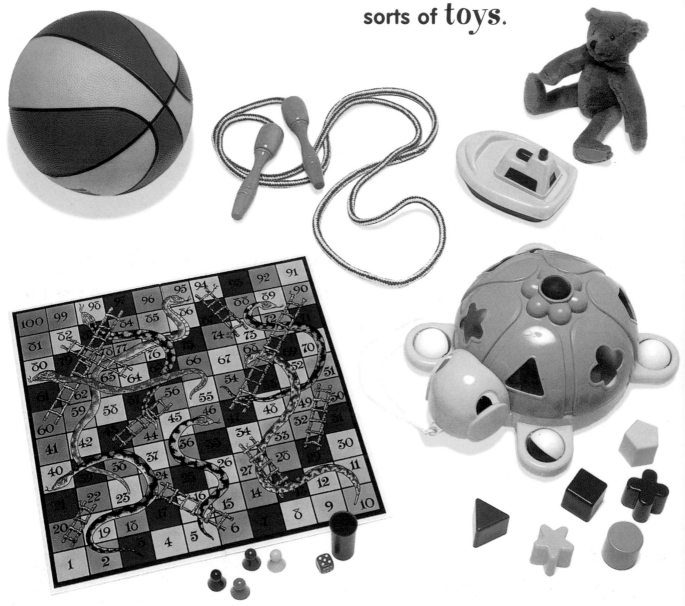

What toys do you **like** to **play** with?

How would **you** play with these toys?

6

Toys are made for **children** of different ages to play with.

Ben's toy car is **soft** and **safe** for babies.

David's car is **plastic** and **strong** and easy for him to push along.

Edward's car is more interesting and has **parts** that **move**.

Baby toys

These toys are especially for **babies**. Would you like to play with them?

Alice likes to **listen** to the **mobile** play a tune and watch the animals move.

Ben likes to take the **hoops** off and put them back on again.

8

Amy is putting each **shape** into the right hole.

All these toys are **plastic**. They are smooth, washable and unbreakable.

Why do you think many **baby** toys are made of plastic?

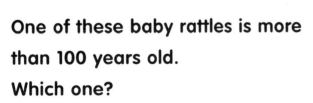

One of these baby rattles is more than 100 years old. Which one?

What differences can you see between the old one and the new one?

Toys to build with

How many different building toys can you think of?

Wooden bricks balance one on top of the other.

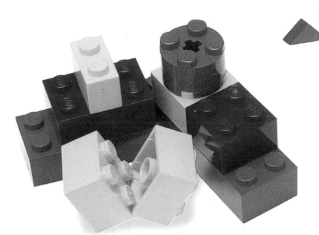

LEGO® bricks lock together firmly.

You can use them to make all sorts of models.

How do you think all these **pieces** fit together?

These pieces of card have been slotted together to make a toy duck. Can you see how? What else could you **make** using the **card**?

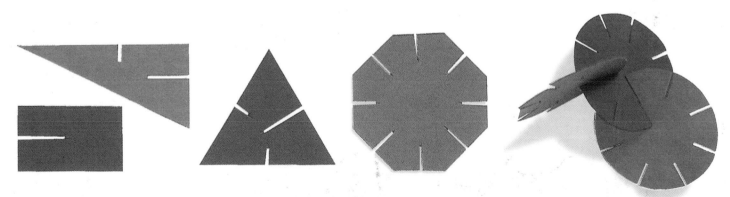

Jigsaw puzzles

A jigsaw is a picture made of **pieces** that fit together.

Jigsaws with lots of pieces can be **difficult**. Which of these four jigsaws would be the most difficult?

Jigsaws for young children have very **simple** shapes.

This jigsaw puzzle has 902 pieces! It is a picture of a famous building in the United States.

Your own jigsaw

Copy these pictures onto two pieces of card. Cut them both into nine pieces. How long does it take you to do each puzzle? Which one takes longer and why?

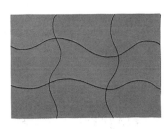

You might cut your pieces out like this.

Fun with puppets

Puppets are good for making up plays and telling stories. You can make them move with your hands and give them voices.

Make a glove puppet

1. Fold a piece of felt in half.

2. Put your hand on the felt and draw a body shape round it.

3. Cut out the puppet shape.

4. Sew round the edges, but leave the bottom open.

5. Give your puppet a face, hair and some clothes.

6. Now put it on your hand and make it move!

You can make every part of this puppet move by moving the bars and pulling its **strings**.

The audience does not actually see these Javanese puppets. They watch their shadows on a large screen.

Try making shadow puppets by using your hands and a bright light.

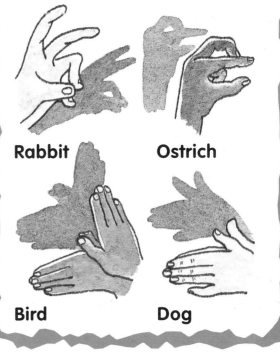

Rabbit   **Ostrich**

Bird   **Dog**

Board games

All board games have **rules** that must be followed.

The **winner** of Snakes and Ladders is the person who reaches the number 100 first.

Players use coloured counters to move around the board.

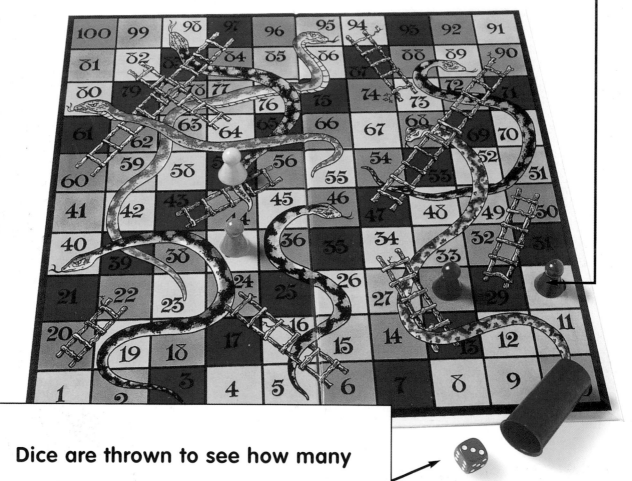

Dice are thrown to see how many squares each player can move.

Design a game

Have fun making up your own **game**. It could be in a jungle, in space or anywhere you want.

Start

1

2

3

4

5

6

7

8

9

10

11

12

13

14

15

16

17

18

19

20

21

22

23

24

25

26

27

2

What kind of counters will you have?

clay shapes

buttons

paper figures

Can you think of any short cuts?

6

13

SWING TO NUMBER 5

What problems might you come across?

SLIP BACK 3 SQUARES

CROCODILE MISS A GO

How will you decide how far you move?

card spinner with colours or numbers

dice

What **shape** will your board be?
What other **ideas** can you think of?

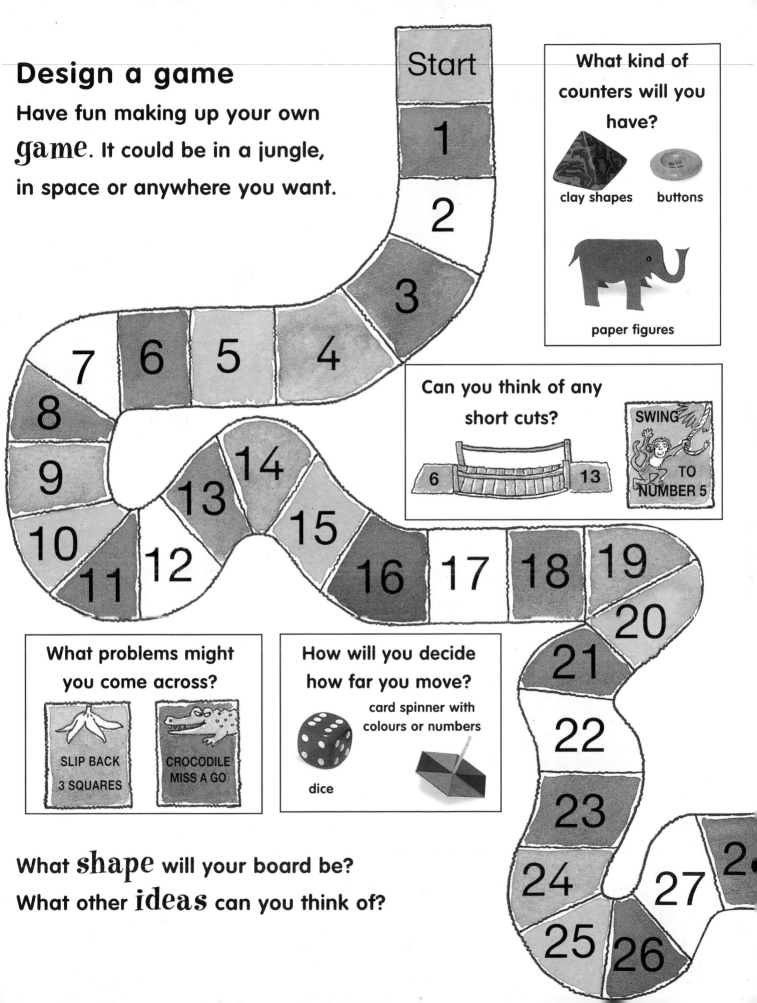

On the move

Some toys are designed to get you on the move.

A skipping rope has to be the right length for your height.

The handles must be comfortable to hold.

This hopper is made of rubber and is filled with air. It is great for bouncing!

When you skateboard, you **roll** over hard, flat ground. You need to **protect** your head, knees and elbows.

A hula hoop only **spins** round when you keep **moving**.

19

All kinds of balls

How many different **ball games** can you think of?
Do you know what these balls are used for?

Balls can be used for **kicking, bouncing, rolling** and **catching**.

A hard baseball flies through the air very fast and you need a **padded glove** to catch it.

This ball is covered in **cloth** and **sticks** to the Velcro on the bat.

eye opener

Throw a round ball onto the same spot several times. It bounces in the same direction.

It is difficult to guess how an oval ball will bounce. Why do you think that is?

Favourite toys

Do you have a **favourite** toy?

Teddy has lots of **stuffing** to make him feel firm. His legs and arms **move**.

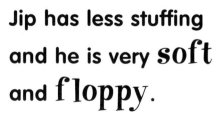

Jip has less stuffing and he is very **soft** and **floppy**.

Russian dolls are made of **wood** and painted brightly. They fit inside each other.

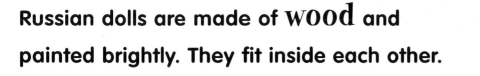

This doll is about 100 years old. Her head is made of china and her body is stuffed. She has real hair.

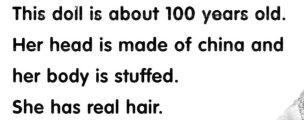

Many modern dolls are plastic and have nylon hair. Which doll would you rather play with?

Playing with Water

Which of these toys would be good for water play?

What are they made of? Would they float or sink?

This toy is lots of fun in the water. What do you think happens when water is poured in?

You can look at this book in the bath because it is waterproof and it floats.

Make one boat from a cardboard box and one from a plastic food tray.

Float them both in water. Which one floats for longer?

Kites

Kites are toys to play with on a windy day. They are made of **light** material and are the right shape to catch the wind.

➡ A long tail helps this diamond-shaped kite to fly.

⬆ A triangle shaped kite is good for flying in a gentle breeze.

➡ A box kite with wings flies well in stronger winds.

Make a kite that flies

You will need:

A rectangle of plastic measuring 40 x 30 cm, cut from a carrier or refuse bag

2 pieces of thin garden cane each measuring 46 cm

Wide double-sided tape

A big needle

Strong thread, including 3 pieces measuring 30 cm each

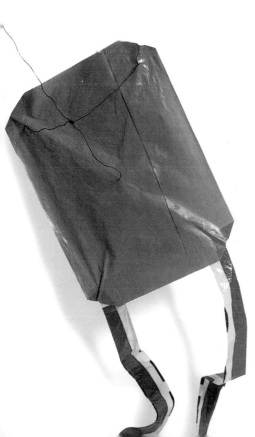

1. Tie a loop in one end of each thread. Stick a piece of tape onto each corner of your plastic sheet.

looped around both sticks

2. Put the loops over the sticks. Peel the backing off the tape. Press the ends of the crossed sticks down.

3. Turn the corners over. Ask an adult to help you get the threads to the other side with a needle.

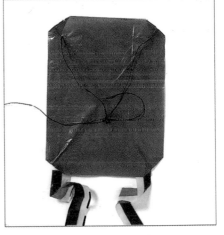

4. Knot the threads together. Tie a very long thread to the knot. Stick on long plastic strips as tails.

5. See how your kite flies!
Make your tails as long as possible.
What happens when they are too short?

Amazing toys

Toys are not always what they **first** seem to be!

This **cuddly** pig is really a hot water bottle cover.

This rocking chair is really **tiny**. It is just right for a dolls house.

This dinosaur has a **baby** that pops out of the **egg** on her back! Can you see what else happens when Dino and her baby get **wet** in the bath water?

A boomerang comes **back** to you when you **throw** it.

This one is made of special **soft** material, so that you can throw it indoors.

Now, try to think up some amazing designs for toys yourself!

Index